D0272810

POSTCARD

Dear Reader,

My name is Edward Marshall Senior. I have four grandchildren – I call them Chillers, and they call me Grandude. I live in a very normal house on a very normal street, but when my Chillers come to stay we go on adventures that are far from normal! Sometimes things get a little bit out of hand . . . but everything always works out fine in the end. Come and join us on an adventure!

Yours sincerely,

Grandude

PUFFIN BOOKS

UK | USA | Canada | Ireland | Australia | India | New Zealand | South Africa

Puffin Books is part of the Penguin Random House group of companies whose addresses can be found at global.penguinrandomhouse.com.

 Penguin Random House UK

First published 2019
001

Copyright © MPL Communications Ltd, 2019
Written by Paul McCartney
Illustrations by Kathryn Durst
The moral right of the author has been asserted

Printed in China
A CIP catalogue record for this book is available from the British Library
ISBN: 978-0-241-37565-5

All correspondence to: Puffin Books, Penguin Random House Children's, 80 Strand, London WC2R 0RL

To every single one of my lovely family – P.M.

For Annabella, Owen and Charlotte. And for their amazing Grandude and Grandudette – my parents! – K.D.

Hey Grandude!

Written by
Paul McCartney

Illustrated by
Kathryn Durst

PUFFIN

Lucy and Tom
and Em and Bob were spending
a weekend with their grandad.

Today was one of those days when
nothing felt quite right.

Lucy

Tom

cookies

It was grey and drizzly, and everybody
was grumpy Bnd too bored to be bothered.

"Cheer up, Chillers!" said Grandude, and he pulled out a pile of postcards from the back pocket of his trousers.

"Look at these!"

Em

Bob

Em picked out a postcard with a picture of a sandy beach
and sparkling blue waters.

"I wish we could go there, Grandude," she said.

"Well, let's see what we can do!"
Grandude reached into his coat pocket and took out a shiny compass.
He gave the compass a rub and waved it over the postcard.
The needle started to spin round and round . . .

See the compass needle spin, let the magic fun begin!

Then in a flash of magic . . .

Zing, bang, sizzle... everything changed!

The children were standing on a golden beach, with little waves tickling their toes. The water felt beautifully cool.

"We're on the beach from the postcard!" Bob laughed as he splashed in the sea.

But the magic compass hadn't finished yet! Huge flying fish leapt from the sea. "Hey, Grandude!" they called.

"It's a school of flying fish!" said Grandude. "Come on, Chillers – let's go for a ride!"

"A school?" whispered Lucy. "I hope we don't have to do any homework!"

They skimmed across shimmering blue waves on the backs of the flying fish, before coming to rest again on the hot sand.

They built sandcastles and then lay beneath a coconut tree, eating ice cream.

The memory of their grey, grumpy day was completely washed away and they were perfectly happy . . .

until . . .

"Ouch!" cried Bob.

A little crab scuttled across the beach.

"That crab pinched my toe!"

Oh no! Suddenly lots of little crabs were scurrying out of the sea, heading straight towards Grandude and the children!

"Hey, Grandude!" said Em. "Can we go somewhere a little less . . ."
"Pinchy! Yes, I think we'd better hop it!" said Grandude.

He quickly waved the magic compass over another postcard.
This one had a picture of a cowboy.

See the compass needle spin,
let the magic fun begin!

The magic flashed and sparkled. And once again . . .

Zing, bang, Sizzle ... everything changed!

Grandude and the children found themselves
in a desert valley with spiky green cactuses.

A cowboy galloped towards them on a beautiful spotted horse.

"Hey, Grandude!" called the cowboy, waving his hat in the air.

"Wow, what a handsome Appaloosa!" said Grandude, admiring the horse.

"Appa-Lucy?" asked Em.

"No, that's the kind of horse it is – nothing to do with me!" said Lucy.

Grandude gave a whistle and five more horses came galloping up.
He helped each of the children on to a horse, and they raced
together through the valley.

"Whee!" cried Bob.

"Faster!" yelled Lucy.

But what was that cloud of dust on the horizon?

Oh no! A herd of wild buffalo was rushing straight towards them. The canyon echoed with the sound of a hundred hooves.

Before they could ride to safety, Tom's horse reared and he tumbled to the ground.

"Hold on, Tom," shouted Grandude,
snatching a rope from the cowboy's saddle.

With a twirl, he lassoed Tom
and hauled him on to his horse.

"Ride, Chillers!" cried Grandude.
"As fast as you can!"

They cleared the stampede – just in time!

"Hey, Grandude," panted Tom.
"Perhaps we could go somewhere
a little less . . ."

"Stampy! Yes, good idea!" said Grandude.
"And I think I need to cool down!"

Once again, he whipped out his magic compass
and waved it over a postcard.

See the compass needle spin,
let the magic fun begin!

Before the children could see the picture,
magic sparkled and flashed. And in the blink of an eye . . .

Zing, bang, sizzle . . . everything changed!

They found themselves high on a hill in the afternoon sun.

The children laughed as they rolled in sweet-smelling wild flowers that seemed to stretch forever. Grandude pulled out his trusty guitar and began strumming a song.

"Hey, Grandude!" mooed some friendly cows, their bells tinkling along to the tune.

Grandude drew a small telescope from his pocket
and they took turns looking at the snow-capped peaks.

But soon they heard a rumbling sound . . .

Oh no!

"Hey, Grandude! Look!" yelled Lucy
as she peered through the telescope.

A huge wall of snow was sliding down
from the mountains above . . .

AVALANCHE!

"Quick, Chillers!" cried Grandude.

"Jump!"

Just before the wave of snow reached them, Grandude and the children leapt on to one of the friendly cows.

"Up, Cow, up!" Grandude cried.

Magic swirled from the compass, lifting them all higher and higher off the ground . . .

. . . sailing them safely through the sky,
with the sea of snow rushing beneath them.

"Swiss cows are exceptionally
good fliers!" said Grandude.

Now, riding a flying cow is a lot of fun,
but it had been a very long day.

"Hey, Grandude!" said Lucy with a yawn.
"Maybe we could go somewhere a little more . . ."

"Sleepy!" said Grandude with a chuckle.
"That sounds like a very good idea!"

This time, instead of a postcard, Grandude pulled a photograph of his own house from his pocket.

Magic compass- one more spin, it's time for **bedtime** to begin!

He waved his compass over it, making the magic sparkle and spin.

And just like that . . .

Zing, bang, Sizzle . . . they were back in Grandude's living room.

And the compass hadn't finished yet!

With a final flash of magic, the children were changed and ready for bed – their teeth were brushed, their faces were washed and they were all tucked up tight.

And in five minutes flat Tom and Bob and Lucy and Em

were fast asleep . . .